Disney
FROZEN FEVER
Read-Along
STORYBOOK AND CD

This is the story of how Queen Elsa surprised
Princess Anna with the best birthday ever.
You can read along with me in your book.
You will know it is time to turn the page
when you hear this sound. . . .
Let's begin now.

Printed in the United States of America

First Paperback Edition, November 2015   10 9 8 7 6 5 4 3 2 1

Library of Congress Control Number: 2015942414

ISBN 978-1-4847-4197-9

FAC-008598-15261

For more Disney Press fun, visit www.disneybooks.com

Disney PRESS

Los Angeles • New York

It was early morning in the kingdom of Arendelle, and Queen Elsa was hard at work. It was Anna's birthday—the first the sisters had spent together since they were children.

Elsa had been preparing for days. She wanted it to be Anna's best birthday ever!

Elsa waved her hands, and a small ice sculpture appeared on the cake she had made for Anna. It was pretty, but it didn't seem quite right. With a flick of her wrist, she tried again.

"Come on, Elsa. This is for Anna. You can do this."

Behind her, Kristoff smiled reassuringly.

"I just want it to be perfect."

"Speaking of perfect, check this out!"

Kristoff pointed up at a handmade banner he and Sven had made. It read HAPPY BIRTHDAY, ANNA in big colorful letters. But the paint was all drippy.

Elsa looked at the messy banner. It was time to wake Anna, but could she really trust Kristoff to finish the party preparations?

"Kristoff, are you sure I can leave you in charge here? Because I don't want anything to happen to this courtyard."

Kristoff was confident. "Absolutely. What could happen? It's all set."

Just then, they heard munching coming from behind them.

It was Olaf. His cheeks were stuffed with frosting from Anna's birthday cake!

"Olaf, what are you doing?"

"I'm not eating cake."

"Olaf . . ."

"But it's an ice cream cake!"

"And it's for Anna."

Olaf removed the piece from his mouth and shoved it back into Anna's cake.

Suddenly, the kingdom bells began to chime.

"Oh, it's time!" Elsa turned to Kristoff. "Okay. You sure you got this?"

"I'm sure."

All Kristoff had to do was make sure everything stayed in order until the party started. And that nothing got broken. And that Olaf didn't eat any more cake.

How hard could it be?

Up in Anna's bedroom, Elsa found her sister fast asleep.

"*Psst*. Anna. Happy birthday!"

Anna yawned. "It's my birthday."

As Anna realized what she had just said, she sat up, fully awake. "It's my birthday!"

Elsa smiled at her sister. "And it's going to be perfect!"

Elsa gave Anna her first birthday present, a beautiful new green-and-teal dress. With a wave of her hand, Elsa used her magic to add icy sparkles to the dress. Then she picked up some flowers from a nearby vase. With a flick of her wrist, she frosted the flowers onto a pretty new green gown for herself.

Anna looked over their new dresses. "Fancy!"

Suddenly, Elsa sneezed.

Unseen by Anna and Elsa, two tiny snowmen appeared. Elsa's sneeze had accidentally created them! The snowmen dropped to the floor and scampered off.

Elsa sniffed and rubbed her nose.
Smiling, she handed Anna the end of
a string. "Just follow the string!"

Anna eagerly went
wherever the string led.
She followed it
through the halls . . .

and over and
under furniture.

With each stop on the string, Anna discovered a birthday present! There was a beautiful bracelet, a silly Olaf cuckoo clock, and even a painting of the sisters and their friends.

Elsa had really thought of everything! The only problem was her sneezing seemed to be getting worse.

Elsa sneezed and sneezed. And with each sneeze, more mini snowmen appeared, scurrying off one by one, unnoticed by the sisters. . . .

Out in the courtyard, Kristoff, Sven, and Olaf were keeping an eye on the surprise party.

Just then, Olaf heard a noise.

"Hello . . . ?"

The little snowmen created by Elsa's sneezes barreled into the courtyard and began knocking over the party decorations!

Kristoff chased after the snowmen. He couldn't let them destroy Anna's party!

Olaf, on the other hand, was very excited. He hugged the snowmen close. "Little brothers!"

Inside the castle, Anna's birthday
adventure continued. Elsa surprised her
sister with more and more presents!
Anna was so grateful. But
she could tell Elsa wasn't
feeling well.

Soon the birthday string led them out of the castle to the
Oaken's Cloakens and Sauna kiosk in the marketplace. Elsa gave
Anna the biggest and softest of Oaken's cloakens . . . just before
sneezing again!

Oaken popped out from the sauna. He offered Elsa a cold
medicine of his own making.

Anna eagerly accepted the medicine. "We'll take it."

Elsa was starting to feel very dizzy. But there was only one gift left! And it was at the top of Arendelle's clock tower.

The sisters climbed up, up, up.

"Elsa, that's too much. You need to rest!"

But Elsa insisted. At the very top, she gave Anna two beautiful wooden dolls. They looked just like the sisters—the perfect birthday present!

Suddenly, Elsa's cold got the better of her, and she swooned. Anna dropped her presents to keep her sister from falling off the tower.

"Elsa, look at you. You've got a fever. You're burning up."

"I'm sorry, Anna. I just wanted to give you one perfect birthday."

Meanwhile, things in the courtyard were *not* going well.
The mini snowmen had destroyed the decorations.
They had pulled down Kristoff's banner.
And *now* they were preparing to launch themselves at
the cake!

"No, no!" Kristoff blocked the snowmen. Olaf grabbed the banner and rearranged the letters. But he didn't know how to spell.

Kristoff tried to read the new banner. "'Dry Banana Hippy Hat'?"

It was a disaster!

Anna carefully led Elsa back to the castle. As she pushed open the doors to the courtyard, Elsa saw Kristoff, Olaf, and Sven tossing the cake back and forth, trying to keep it away from the little snowmen. Kristoff jumped up onto Sven, and Olaf ran by with the birthday banner.

Anna was focused on Elsa and didn't see anything. But Elsa was horrified. The courtyard was in chaos!

Anna looked up just as Kristoff caught the cake and the birthday banner settled into place. Her face lit up. She had never had a surprise birthday party before. And to her everything looked . . . perfect! But where had all the little snowmen come from?

"Wow!"

Kristoff hopped off Sven and walked up to Anna, birthday cake in hand. "Happy birthday."

Kristoff was so happy to see Anna that he blurted out that he loved her. For a minute, he looked embarrassed. Then he shrugged. "I do."

Anna couldn't believe it. It was all so wonderful! But she was
still worried about Elsa.

Elsa promised she was well enough for at least one piece of
cake. So Sven cut slices for everyone.

The party was perfect, but Anna insisted it was time for Elsa to get some rest. "Okay, to bed with you."

"No, wait, wait. All that's left to do is for the queen to blow the birthday bugle horn."

Elsa grabbed the horn . . . and accidentally sneezed into it! A giant snowball flew out of the end. It sailed across the kingdom!

Upstairs, Anna tucked a very tired Elsa into bed. She made her some hot soup, sat down next to her, and smiled. "Best birthday present ever."

Elsa was confused. "Which one?"

"You letting me take care of you."

Anna's party was over, but Kristoff and Olaf still had one thing to do. Up in the mountains, they knocked on the doors to the ice palace.

The doors swung open. Marshmallow was inside.

Olaf pushed past Marshmallow. "This way, Sludge and Slush and Slide and Ansel and Flake and Fridge and Flurry and Powder and Crystal and Squall and Pack and Sphere and William." Behind Olaf came a trail of little snowgies.

Kristoff sighed and looked at Marshmallow. "Don't ask."